YO-KAI WATCH™

Komasan and Komajiro in the City

Adapted by Kate Howard

Any attempt to replicate Yo-kai behavior would be ill-advised!

SCHOLASTIC INC.

S0-AHE-704

If you purchased this book without a cover, you should be aware that this book is stolen property. It was reported as "unsold and destroyed" to the publisher, and neither the author nor the publisher has received any payment for this "stripped book."

©LEVEL-5/YWP. Produced by Scholastic Inc. under license from LEVEL-5.

Published by Scholastic Inc., *Publishers since 1920.* SCHOLASTIC and associated logos are trademarks and/or registered trademarks of Scholastic Inc.

The publisher does not have any control over and does not assume any responsibility for author or third-party websites or their content.

No part of this publication may be reproduced, stored in a retrieval system, or transmitted in any form or by any means, electronic, mechanical, photocopying, recording, or otherwise, without written permission of the publisher. For information regarding permission, write to Scholastic Inc., Attention: Permissions Department, 557 Broadway, New York, NY 10012.

This book is a work of fiction. Names, characters, places, and incidents are either the product of the author's imagination or are used fictitiously, and any resemblance to actual persons, living or dead, business establishments, events, or locales is entirely coincidental.

ISBN 978-1-338-05828-4

10 9 8 7 6 5 4 3 2 1   17 18 19 20 21

Printed in the U.S.A.   40
First printing 2017

Nate was just an ordinary fifth grader—until he discovered the secret, invisible world of Yo-kai. Yo-kai are mischievous beings who *love* to create problems for the human world.

Got the wrong order at the drive-through? Can't find your homework that you *know* you put in your backpack? A Yo-kai is probably to blame.

Thanks to the Yo-kai Watch, Nate can see and communicate with these magical beings. With the help of his self-proclaimed Yo-kai butler, Whisper, it's Nate's job to befriend the Yo-kai. He often calls upon his Yo-kai pals for help. But first, he has to win over each Yo-kai and get them to trust him.

This is the story of Komasan and Komajiro—two Yo-kai brothers eager to make their way in the big city.

CHAPTER 1

HERE'S KOMASAN!

"HERE'S YOUR ICE CREAM!"

Nate Adams reached across the counter and took his ice-cream cone from the cashier at mogmog Burgers. Before he could take his first lick, he stopped short and stared at the swirl on top of his cone. "This is ... wrong!"

This is ... wrong!

"Hey, what's the matter, Nate?" asked Whisper. Whisper was the guide who helped Nate understand the mysterious world of Yo-kai.

"There's some missing!" Nate growled. "This swirl is clearly too short. It's supposed to have four spirals. Mine's only got three!"

"It still tastes the same," said Whisper.

"I paid two bucks for this and I demand two bucks' worth of ice cream!" Nate mumbled. "Whisper, it's got to be a Yo-kai pulling some sort of scam."

Whisper laughed. "Impossible. No way."

But Nate wasn't convinced. Yo-kai were hidden everywhere, and when something went sideways, there was usually a Yo-kai involved.

Frowning, Nate swept the Yo-kai Watch over the restaurant.

Suddenly, a small, white creature came into view. Nate pointed at the creature, who was merrily licking a spiral off another customer's ice-cream cone. "There!"

The little Yo-kai stopped mid-lick. "What in tarnation?" he exclaimed. "You can see me?"

"Yeah." Nate shrugged. Most people couldn't see Yo-kai and didn't even know they existed. But thanks to the Yo-kai Watch, Nate could see the mischievous creatures.

The little Yo-kai hopped off the counter and joined Whisper and Nate at their table. "I can't rightly believe y'all can see me. City folk are real whizzes."

"Who are you?" Nate asked.

"Name's Komasan," the Yo-kai said. "Glad to meet y'all!"

"Y'all?" Nate repeated.

"That there's country talk," Whisper explained. "He's not from around here."

Nate glared at the Yo-kai. "Well, that doesn't give him the right to eat my ice cream. Around here that's called stealing!"

Komasan hung his head sadly. "Oh my swirls . . ." His

eyes grew wide with hunger when a server walked past with a platter of ice-cream cones.

"So what's up with your obsession with ice cream?" Nate asked.

Whisper chuckled. "To a Yo-kai, nothing is more delicious than someone else's ice cream. Some think that the ice cream of others simply tastes better."

Komasan nodded. "When I see that rich, creamy, sweet goodness . . . oh my." Komasan stared at the swirled top of Whisper's head, which was twitching and wiggling in a very ice cream–like way. "I can't rightly control myself!" Komasan cried. He leaped up and chomped at the top of Whisper's head.

Nate grinned. "You know that's Whisper's head, right?"

Whisper giggled. "That feels surprisingly good!"

Komasan began to tell the story of his ice-cream problem. "It all started when I was fixin' to meet my brother at the Japanese gardens. I waited and waited for many days. But Komajiro never showed up. Made me ornery. One day a strange festival came to the park. It was a hoot just to watch but . . . oh my swirls, there was one thing I found downright irresistible!"

"You stole their ice cream?" Nate asked.

I looked everywhere to get me some ice cream!

Komasan sighed. "There was nothing on this great green earth that I wanted more than to try some of that cool, sweet confection! I searched high and low. I looked everywhere to get me some. And once I tried it, I couldn't stop. When I eat ice cream, I'm happier than a newborn lamb in spring." Komasan happily licked at Whisper's head again.

"Dude, that's not ice cream," Nate said, nudging the little Yo-kai off Whisper.

Komasan shrugged. "I thought maybe it just went sour."

"I don't get it," Nate said. "Don't you have ice cream in the country? I still don't understand why you're here."

"I went back to the garden, but it done got all torn up," Komasan said. "I was madder than a wet hen, but there was nothin' left to do. So I came to the city! Ever since I got here, I've been busier than a one-armed paper hanger."

"What'd he say?" Nate leaned in to ask Whisper.

"Your guess is as good as mine," Whisper said. "Frankly, I don't speak bumpkin."

"Now, every time I get a hankerin' for some of that heavenly ice cream, I come here," Komasan said dreamily. "They gots plenty of it and people sure don't mind sharin'."

Whisper cringed. "If he stays here any longer, Nate, ice-cream losses will be catastrophic."

Nate stood up. "Let's show Komasan around the city! Maybe he'll find a place he likes to hang out."

So Nate and Whisper spent the whole day showing Komasan around. Komasan *loved* their adventure. The city was filled with so many new, amazing things he had never seen before in the country.

"This city is as fine as a frog's hair split four ways," Komasan declared happily.

"Where do you want to go next, Komasan?" Nate asked, stepping onto an escalator. He looked over, but Komasan was no longer beside him. "Komasan?"

"Oh my swirls," Komasan whispered nervously from the bottom of the escalator. He was afraid to step onto the mysterious moving walkway. He stuck his foot out, and then pulled it away and hurried in the opposite direction.

Komasan's next adventure involved a revolving door. "Oh my *swirls*!" the little Yo-kai gasped as he spun around and around inside the door.

Komasan had a *lot* to learn about city life. There were many, many things the little Yo-kai had never seen before. Nate and Whisper showed him how to make his way through a crowd of people, how to cross a busy street, and even how a public restroom worked. The country critter was amazed by everything.

"Oh my! Is there a Yo-kai in there?" Komasan asked, staring at the toilet as it flushed automatically.

"It's just an automatic toilet," Nate explained.

Whisper giggled. "How did he survive without us?"

Nate sighed and shook his head as they made their way down the street. "I never knew sightseeing could be so stressful."

Suddenly, Nate and Whisper heard Komasan cry out from somewhere nearby. They looked around, trying to figure out where their new friend had gone.

"I'm nervouser than a long-tailed cat in a room full of rocking chairs!" Komasan's voice echoed from far away.

Nate and Whisper raced down an alley, following the sound of Komasan's voice. The little Yo-kai was cowering under a shadowy figure. It was Roughraff, the tough-talking, bad-boy Yo-kai!

"I've been watching you, country bumpkin," Roughraff growled. "Hand over all your money!"

Nate and Whisper raced toward their new friend. "Komasan!"

"Rats," said Roughraff, spotting Nate. He raced away. "See ya . . ."

"Are you okay, Komasan?" Nate asked.

Komasan sniffled. "I been staggerin' around this city like a blind horse in a pumpkin patch. I've a mind to change my ways."

"It just takes some time to get used to the city," Nate said. "Roughraff won't bother you again."

"Still," Komasan said. "I'm afraid it's time for me to go home. It's more peaceful in the country. Life is simple there. Good-bye, Nate, and, uh . . ." He glanced at Whisper. "Whis-cream?"

"Whis-*per*!" Whisper corrected him.

"Oh." Komasan sighed. "Y'all take care now. Here's my Yo-kai Medal, Nate. Bless your heart for everything."

"Komasan," Nate said. "I think we may actually miss you."

"Oh my swirls!" Komasan said happily.

"Oh my swirls!" Nate replied.

Nate and Whisper escorted Komasan to the train station and waved good-bye as the little Yo-kai hopped onboard the train.

"Good-bye, y'all!" Komasan called.

"Maybe we'll see him again sometime," Nate said.

As they made their way back home, Nate noticed Komasan had left his backpack in the alley. So he pulled out Komasan's Yo-kai Medal and popped it into his watch.

Holding the watch high in the air, Nate cried, "Come

on out, my friend! Calling Komasan! Yo-kai Medal, do your thing!"

Komasan appeared out of thin air. He looked terrified. "Well, I'm fit to be tied! Why am I back in the city?!"

Why am
I back in
the city?!

Nate chuckled. "I called you using the medal. You left your backpack here."

Komasan moaned when he realized he was back in the city again. "I feel lower than a snake in snowshoes, y'all."

Dear Mama,

It's me, Komasan. I done reckoned that coming to the city would make me happier than a pig in slop. But now I see that the city is all hat and no cattle. I just want to come home, Mama . . .

KOMASAN

CHAPTER 2

KOMASAN WAS GLUM. He just couldn't figure out how anything worked in the big city, and he longed to return to his simple life in the country.

Then one day, shortly after Nate called him back to the city, Komasan heard a familiar voice call out, "Brother?"

Komasan looked up and gasped. "Komajiro! Well, look who the cat dragged in. It's my little brother, Komajiro! What in tarnation?"

"I've been searching high and low and far and wide for you, brother," said Komajiro. "A friendly face is scarcer than hen's teeth 'round here."

Komasan nodded. "You said it, brother."

"But now that I found you, everything's right as rain!"

Everything's right as rain!

Komajiro cheered. "My big brother is here to protect me from the big, scary city."

Komasan scratched his head. He wasn't so sure about that . . .

"You must be handier than a pocket on a shirt at city livin' by now," said Komajiro.

"Uh . . ." Komasan gulped. "Sure . . . sure I am."

Komajiro whooped. "*Hoo-eee!* Then let's get crackin', brother! I want to see everything!"

"Alrighty then," said Komasan. "I can learn ya what I know. Your big brother'll show you 'round."

As they set off to explore all the new places Nate

had shown him, Komasan warned his brother, "Life in the city is faster than all get out. Danger lurks 'round every corner. Listen up and keep your eyes peeled."

He stopped at an escalator.

Komajiro stared. "What's this?"

"Gee willikers," Komasan said, then blinked. "Looking at these moving stairs too long'll make you greener than a turnip head. Listen to me, brother. It's all in the timing." He carefully reached his toe toward the escalator. "You gotta get it just right, or else it's gonna go all kindsa wrong for ya. Sometimes it helps to count. One . . . t-two . . ." He braced himself.

Suddenly, Komajiro yelled to him from the top of the escalator. "You coming or what, brother?"

Komasan gasped when he realized his brother wasn't afraid of the escalator at *all*. "Huh? Oh my swirls! I don't think I know him anymore ..."

Dear Mama,
 I miss you like all get out. Komajiro and I are living high on the hog here in the city. Too bad sometimes Komajiro gets as lost as last year's Easter egg ...
                                KOMASAN

CHAPTER 3

URBAN LIVING

"**N**OW WHERE IS THAT RASCAL?" Komasan muttered, searching for his brother in a crowd of people.

"Komasan!" came his brother's sad cry. He was riding through the crowd on top of someone's head. "Help me! How do you stop this thing?"

Where is that rascal?

"I'm stuck!" Komajiro yelled. "I don't know what to do!"

"All right, don't get your cows all running. I'm coming!" Komasan called out. "Do what I do, Komajiro, or you'll be flatter than a flitter. You have to get a rhythm going. One . . . two . . . one . . . two. It's a little game I call head surfing!"

Komasan hopped from head to head, floating over the top of the crowd like he was riding a wave on a surfboard. It was scary, but Komasan knew he had to show his brother how it was done.

I'm coming!

"Gee whiz!" Komajiro sighed. "My own brother's cooler than the other side of the pillow!"

Following Komasan's lead, Komajiro began jumping from head to head, pretending he was surfing, too.

"Golly. He caught on right quick," Komasan said, surprised. "Could it be that Komajiro is becoming a city slicker without my knowing it? Oh my!" He called, "Keep going, brother! Don't forget the rhythm."

Suddenly, the head Komasan had been balancing on began to move. "Whoa!" he yelped, trying to keep his balance.

A moment later, Komasan realized something. He was trapped in someone's fancy hairdo! "Well, this is a fine how-do-you-do . . . now *I'm* stuck. Komajiro, help!"

I'm stuck!

Once they were back on solid ground, Komajiro put his arm around his brother. "The city is such an amazing place. Oh, brother... I can't wait to learn even more from you!"

The city is such an amazing place...

Dear Mama,
   It's me again, komasan. How are you?
   My brother is awful excited by the big city. He's cuter than a sack full of puppies, but he sure is a handful. We're thick as flies on a dog's back, so don't you worry about us.
   This city's got more folks than you can beat back with a stick. Makes me dizzier than a monkey on a carousel!

KOMASAN

CHAPTER 4

THE TURNSTILE

"**O**H MY SWIRLS!" Komajiro said as he and Komasan entered the train station in the center of the big city. "Brother, what's *that* highfalutin thing?"

He and his brother stared as a human walked through the ticket gate. The gate swung open and closed like the mouth of some kind of giant, metal creature.

Komasan swallowed. "It's called a swing-door-beeper," he told his brother, making up the first name he could think of. "You can tell by just looking at it."

"Holy moly, big brother," Komajiro said. He was impressed by how smart his big brother was about all sorts of stuff in the big city. "Have you ever used it?"

"Me? Of course!" Komasan lied. "It's a snap. Come on!"

Komajiro smiled. "Aw, brother, I wouldn't trade you for a farm in Georgia!"

"Aw shucks, y'all," Komasan muttered to himself as he approached the ticket gate. "I'm a gosh-darned fibber. I'm shaking in my boots! I got to rustle myself up some courage."

Komasan stared at the metal doors, swinging open and shut to let passengers go through. "Don't worry your little head 'bout it, brother."

"Komasan, wait up!" Komajiro called.

Komasan stood, unmoving, at the gates. "Well, time's a-wastin'." He stepped forward, ready to face the evil metal jaws as they snapped angrily open and closed. "Holy smokes, I'm feeling hotter than a June bride." He suddenly wondered if he could get trapped in the gates. "Oh my swirls!"

Holy smokes!

"Are you callin' my bluff, swing-door-beeper?" Komasan growled. Then he took a step backward. "Somehow, this swing-door-beeper knows I'm not city folk! It knows I'm country through and through."

Komasan fell to his knees. "You bested me this time, swing-door-beeper."

Just then, Komajiro strode toward the gates with a pass card in his hand. "Check this out, brother," he said, waving the pass in the air. "This thing gets you through the gate."

"Stop, Komajiro!" Komasan called, watching his brother bravely step up to the swinging gate. "Wait! That thing's as crooked as a barrel full of fishhooks!"

But Komajiro didn't stop. He didn't wait. He just placed the card in front of the gate, and the doors swung open for him.

"Check me out, bro! I'm in!" Komajiro called to his brother from the other side.

Komasan stared at him. "What happened, Komasan? Don'tcha have a MetroPass?" Komajiro asked.

"Well, I'll be," Komasan whispered. "I'm so surprised you could knock my eyes out with a stick. It's not 'cause I'm country after all."

Komasan smiled at his brother. He tried to act like he had known about the card reader the whole time.

"Ah, little brother, you're still so young and unwisdomly. City folks get their cards put right inside their bodies."

Komajiro stared at him in amazement. "That's so cool! Can I get that, too?"

City folks get their cards right inside their bodies!

"Slow down, little brother," said Komasan. "Give it time. You'll be ready one day."

"I can't wait!" cheered Komajiro. "I'll make you proud, big brother! You'll see." Then he turned and ran up the stairs to the train platform.

"Komajiro, where are you off to?" Komasan called out. He raced after his little brother... but just as he

was about to run through, the gates slammed shut!
Komasan flew backward.

Sometimes it seemed like his brother was learning about the big city a whole lot faster than he was...

Dear Mama,
    Mama, did you know that city folk are all sortsa crazy? They walk around all day jabbering to themselves. And always with those newfangled ear warmers. Why do they do that? Why? Why?
    Good-bye for now, but I'll write again directly!

KOMASAN

CHAPTER 5

EAR WARMERS

"**B**ROTHER!" Komajiro cried, pointing to a human walking past. "Why do the city folk talk so much while they're walking?"

"So you noticed that too, Komajiro?" asked Komasan. "It's because they're all losing their doggone minds! They got more problems than a math book. Even to an experienced city dweller like me, it don't make no sense."

A smartphone?

"But isn't that thing on their ears a smartphone?" Komajiro asked.

"Huh?" Komasan said. "A smartphone?"

"You have to admit that smartphones are useful," Komajiro pointed out. "It's so convenient to be able to talk to your friends from anywhere. I'm totally into it."

Komasan had no idea what his brother was talking about. *Smartphones?* What kind of crazy talk was that? "Smart . . . phone?"

Komajiro pulled out his own phone and frowned. "Darn it all . . ." he said, staring at the screen. He was expecting an important phone call. "I can't get a signal here. No bars, man."

"Signal . . . ? Uh . . ." Komasan felt like his brother was speaking another language.

Komajiro turned to Komasan. "Brother, do you know where I can get better reception 'round here?"

"Darn tootin' if I know," Komasan lied.

"Well?" Komajiro prompted. "Where?"

"Um . . . over there?" Komasan began running down the sidewalk, pointing at nothing in particular.

Komajiro raced after him. He knew his brother would show him just where he needed to go.

"There's more bars there than you can swing a cat at!" Komasan said.

There's more bars there than you can swing a cat at!

"Wow, brother," Komajiro said, impressed. "You really are up on your cell phone plans."

"'Course I am, brother. I am like a bar hunter. I can scare up some good signals for ya anytime you want," Komasan said, hoping his brother would believe him.

"You're so smart!" Komajiro said happily. "I never knew there was such a thing as good signals and bad signals."

Komasan nodded. "Sure, it's a fact. The waves over here are smooth and delicious. Trust me, I know good waves when I see 'em."

As they raced down the street, Komajiro's phone began to ring. "Oh! I'm getting a call. Brother, this is the call I was waiting for!" He stopped short and answered.

"Hey? What's up? Uh, hang on. I get terrible reception around here."

Komajiro put the call on hold and waved to Komasan. "Bye, brother, I'll see you at home. I'm off to hang out with my friends now."

Komasan watched, jealous, as his brother turned and headed off without him. "Ah, okay . . ."

As soon as Komajiro was gone, Komasan shook his head. "I don't know what's happening to him . . ." With a sigh, he set off toward home.

Then he grinned. Country folk could find the silver lining in any situation. There was a skip in Komasan's step. "Looks like I'm only fixin' dinner for one tonight!"

Dear Mama,
    Don't worry a hair on your little head. Komajiro is getting the hang of city living just fine! The big city is more confusing than a giraffe in rain boots . . . but I won't let nothin' hurt my little brother.
                        KOMASAN

CHAPTER 6

 LOW-BUDGET VITTLES

"**T**HIS IS WHERE THE CITY FOLK get the best fast food," Komasan told his brother as they walked toward mogmog Burgers the next day.

Komajiro gasped as he stared at the shiny, colorful restaurant. "So you've tried it, then? I can't wait!"

In fact, Komasan had had some difficulties ordering

39

fast food. "Huh? Well, it's not like I haven't NOT tried it before." He cleared his throat. "There are some truths you need to hear about fast food before we rustle some up. Hush now. What the folks call 'fast food'..." He paused.

Komajiro stared at him, amazed by how much his brother knew about the big city. "Uh-huh?"

"It ain't exactly fast," Komasan said. "It's just yummy, low-budget vittles. However, if you're fixin' to buy yourself a simple meal, they say... '*Would you like fries with that?*' and '*It's cheaper if you make it a meal combo!*'"

Komasan grunted, thinking about his past visits to fast-food restaurants. None of them had ended with him getting what he'd meant to order. "They jabber on and on and on about all the choices, and your brain ends up emptier than a winter rain barrel. In the end, you have no darn tootin' idea what to choose at all. It's humiliating."

Komajiro nodded thoughtfully. That didn't sound too bad to him! He and his smart big brother could handle anything the big city folk threw at them. "We'll have to show them how tough us country folk are!"

"Just remember," Komasan warned. "Any time they

say '*With that*,' it's a trap! We will buy nothing but a single drink!"

Komajiro pumped his fist. "They can't fool us!"

The two brothers stepped inside the restaurant. Komasan pointed at his head. "These Yo-kai leaves make humans think we're one of them. If we wear one, to them, we'll look like humans."

"How convenient!" Komajiro said, patting his Yo-kai leaf.

When the clerk was ready, Komasan stepped up to the counter. "Follow my lead, brother!" he whispered.

These Yo-kai leaves make us look like humans.

Komajiro nodded seriously.

The clerk looked at Komasan and smiled sweetly. "How may I help you, sir?"

Komasan leaned toward his brother. "See her smile? It's a trick. These people are more crooked than a barrel of fishhooks."

"I'll be careful, brother," Komajiro promised. "They can't fool us!"

Stay strong, brother!

A second clerk waved Komajiro toward a different register. "Hello, sir. I can take you over here."

Komajiro looked at her, then back at his brother. He said, "Uh, I guess I'll go over there?"

Komasan nodded. "Stay strong, brother!"

The first clerk smiled at Komasan. "Well, you're in luck, sir. Today we're running a limited time special." She held up a flyer for the BIG Burger Meal. "Would you like one?"

"U-u-uh . . ." Komasan stammered.

The clerk kept smiling at him. Her smile was so pretty, and the burger looked so juicy and delicious. Suddenly, Komasan blurted, "I will take it."

The clerk's smile widened. "Good choice, sir. Would you like to add an apple pie or an ice cream for just a dollar? Just smell the delicious aroma."

Komasan looked away. He tried not to be tempted by the wonderful pie smell. But he was having trouble keeping his wits about him. The clerk was so beautiful, and she had so many nice things to offer!

"I will take it," Komasan groaned.

"Very good, sir!" she said happily.

Next the clerk held up a cup of soft-serve ice cream. Right there in front of Komasan was a big cup full of tempting, creamy, sweet swirls of ice cream! "Would you like to make your pie à la mode with this scrumptious ice-cream topping?"

Then she dangled an ice cream–shaped key chain in front of him. "You also get this limited-edition key chain!"

Komasan's eyes went wide. "I will take it."

The clerk nodded happily. "And why not make it a

I'll take it!

feast with our new Steak Burger...which comes with a free toy!"

A few minutes later, Komajiro joined his brother at their table. He gaped at the heaping tray of treats in front of Komasan. "What happened to our plan, brother?"

Komasan moaned and hung his head. "She done played me like a banjo!"

"Why?" asked Komajiro.

"I tried to resist!" Komasan howled. "But everything sounded so good, and she was smiling at me, and sure as a cat's got climbing gear, I got it all. And I didn't want it. I didn't want any of it. Just look at all this stuff!"

She done played me like a banjo!

"Amazing, brother!" Komajiro said, his eyes filled with wonder. "You are so brave and adventurous."

"Huh?" Komasan asked.

"Only someone courageous would dare to try all those unusual foods of debatable quality. I hope I can be just like you one day, brother," Komajiro said earnestly.

Komasan managed a weak smile. "Well . . . I'm glad that I was able to set a good example."

Dear Mama,
    It's me, Komasan. Komajiro is so young and impressionable. I am so glad that I can be here to guide him through life.
    At this point, I am a doggone expert when it comes to the big city. But Komajiro still has a tough row to hoe. Tomorrow, we're off to visit the observation tower!

KOMASAN

CHAPTER 7

THE MAGIC FLOOR

"**K**OMAJIRO, THIS IS QUITE A TREAT," Komasan said as they walked toward the tallest tower in the city. Komasan was planning to take his brother up to the top of the tower for a view out over the whole city and beyond. "I bet you ain't never seen nothin' like this back in the country."

Komajiro looked down at his phone. "Looks great," he muttered.

"Did you know you can see all the way to the end of the world from the top?" Komasan asked. He began to tell his brother about all the cool things they would be able to see from that high up.

But Komajiro scanned his phone and shook his head. "Um, not really. You can only see maybe fifteen or twenty miles, tops."

"How disappointing," Komasan grumbled. He and Komajiro stepped onto a crowded elevator.

The elevator raced toward the sky. "Oh my swirls!" Komasan cheered. The elevator was made of glass, and they could see the whole world as they shot upward. "This is cooler than an April shower! At this rate, we're gonna get all the way to the sun in no time! Golly. Everything looks so itty-bitty. It's like ants live there."

Komajiro laughed. "Oh, brother, you know we can't really get to the sun in this elevator, don't you? We'll reach the observatory in fifty seconds, and of course the people on the ground will look small at this height."

"Sure," Komasan said, and then nodded, trying to act casual. "I knew that."

Komasan and Komajiro got off the elevator. "Ooh! We're here, brother." Komasan raced out to the edge of the observation deck. "Oh my swirls! Is that the same mountain we got at home? It's so purty."

Komajiro peered at his phone. "According to this, our home is on the exact opposite side. Over there."

"Oh," Komasan said. "Still . . . amazing!" He ran to the other side of the observation deck. But he screeched to a stop when he realized the floor he was walking on was *see-through*! "What in tarnation, brother?! The floor is invisible! How is it holding us in place? What is happening? What do I do?"

We should get off this magic floor!

"We should get off this magic floor," Komasan went on. "So we don't fall through."

Komajiro laughed as he read all about the floor on his phone. "That's not possible. That's four layers of foot-thick tempered glass. It can hold an elephant."

"Uh, what a relief," Komasan said, trying to make it seem like he already knew that.

Suddenly, something amazing caught his eye. "Oh, golly. Look! Souvenirs! Gnats spats, brother, this water bottle looks just like the tower! Brother, shall we...?" He paused, and then muttered to himself, "I gotta act cooler than a mule chewin' on bumblebees." Aloud, he said, "Komajiro, are you thirsty? I'd be right proud to buy you one!"

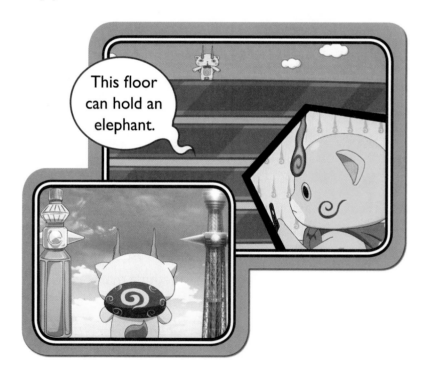

But Komajiro opened his bag and pointed inside. "I already bought some before we left. Down at the bottom of the tower they're cheaper, you know."

Komasan scratched his head. He did *not* know that! "Uh, really? Uh, thank y'all . . ."

The sun was starting to set. The moon was high in the sky, and the stars had begun to come out.

Komasan sighed sadly. "Komajiro wasn't impressed at all . . ." Then he caught sight of something marvelous. Komasan gasped and pointed.

"Are you all right, brother?" Komajiro asked.

"Did you see that?" Komasan said, pointing.

A shooting star slashed across the sky.

"Oh my swirls!" Komajiro whooped. "Well, I'll be . . . that was a shooting star!"

"Did I impress you, Komajiro?" Komasan asked hopefully.

"You found a shooting star!" said Komajiro, amazed. "Brother, I have never been more amazed in my entire life!"

Brother, I have never been more amazed in my entire life!

"R-really?" Komasan asked.

Komajiro nodded and looked at his brother with stars in his eyes. "Someday, I want to be as amazing as you are, brother!"

Dear mama,

It's me, komasan. Today was a good day. The big city don't feel so scary anymore, and I'm feeling right as rain.

But there's one thing that's got me all hot and bothered.

I think the big city is starting to change komajiro. I must admit that komajiro's got the big city all figured out. Sometimes I'm pantin' like an old dog, trying to catch up . . .

KOMASAN

CHAPTER 8

MY COOL BROTHER

"**Yo!**" KOMAJIRO BARKED into his cell phone. "What's up? What's the sitch? Tonight? Yeah, I'm down with that, bro. That place is dope."

Yeah, I'm down with that, bro.

Komasan stared at his little brother like he was going crazy. What in tarnation was he saying into his ear warmer?

"Yeah," Komajiro said into the phone. "For sure. I'll see you there. Later, man!"

"Komajiro, I can't understand one darn thing you're saying," Komasan told him after Komajiro had hung up.

Komajiro laughed, sure his brother had to be kidding. "Brother, I'm going out to see some friends, cool?"

"Uh, Komajiro, where do you go all the time?" Komasan asked. Lately, his brother had been hanging out with friends more and more often. Komasan was starting to feel a little jealous.

"Oh, it's a totally awesome place, brother! There are beautiful lights and everyone dances to the sound of wonderful music."

"Oh, that?" Komasan said, thinking back to all the wonderful festivals he'd been to back in the country. "I've done that before!"

"Wow, big brother!" Komajiro said. "You're amazing! You're always two steps ahead of me."

Komasan smiled sheepishly. "So, can I come dancing, too?"

"For sure," Komajiro said. "Now I can finally introduce you to my friends!"

When they got to the club, Komasan immediately realized he'd never been anywhere like this before. "Oh my swirls!" He gasped, looking around at all the people and spinning lights. Music thumped all around them.

Komasan had never been so overwhelmed in his whole life. But next to him, Komajiro was as cool as a cucumber under a water hose.

"This is, uh—" Komasan began.

"... the club I was telling you about," Komajiro broke in. "Are the clubs you go to like this, too?"

"Uh, yes?" Komasan murmured.

Just then, someone danced over and high-fived Komajiro. "Hey, KJ! Long time no see, buddy!"

"Komajiro," Komasan said, confused. "Who is KJ?"

"Oh, that. It's just what they call me here. KJ is short for Komajiro," his brother explained.

A moment later, a beautiful girl raced over and hugged Komajiro. "Where have you been hiding yourself?" she asked him.

"Tarnation!" Komasan exclaimed.

The girl laughed. "Tarnation? What's that? Sounds totally street."

Komasan blinked and smiled at the girl. "Komajiro, who is this . . . this . . . beauty queen?"

Komajiro grinned. "Yeah, this here's my girlfriend, Sophie."

"Ah!" Sophie said, grinning at Komasan. "So this is your big brother! You were telling me about him. Oh, he's such a trip."

This here's my girlfriend, Sophie.

Komasan bowed. "Pleased to meetcha, ma'am."

"So . . . uh, we're gonna go to the VIP room," Komajiro told his brother as he and Sophie walked away. "But you should totally chill here and have fun. Lates!"

"Little brother's getting stranger than a five-legged worm," Komasan muttered, shaking his head.

Later that night, Komasan watched as his brother deejayed. "Komajiro . . ." he muttered sadly to himself. "I don't know you anymore."

A group of guys danced over to Komajiro. "Your grooves touch my very soul, bro!" one cried.

Komajiro grinned. "Thanks, man!"

Another guy asked, "Hey, KJ. Have you picked out your threads for the dance team contest yet?"

"Of course," Komajiro said. "You trippin'?" He held out a T-shirt with his brother's favorite swirls all over it. "Check this out! I made ones for the whole team."

"No way, man. That thread's cray-cray," said one of the guys. "I ain't wearin' that."

"What are you talking about?" Komajiro blurted. "These shirts are on fleek! It's my brother's all-time favorite design!"

The guys all shook their heads. "I refuse to dress like some sort of country bumpkin!" said one.

The second guy nodded. "You know, it all makes sense now. KJ is just a country boy from the sticks."

"H-h-huh?" Komajiro stuttered. "I ain't no such thing, y'all!"

"*Y'all?*" The third guy laughed, picking Komajiro up and dangling him over the dance floor.

The guys all laughed as Komajiro struggled to break free. "This farm boy's not cool," the first guy said.

Suddenly, Komasan ran over to protect his little brother. "Put him down, y'all."

"Huh?" the three guys said, spinning around to face Komasan.

Komasan held up his fists. "Else you're gonna get a proper whuppin'."

"Who are you anyway?" the second guy demanded.

The third guy laughed. "He's gotta be KJ's country brother."

Komasan stood tall. "That's right, y'all! And dont'cha talk bad about the country, neither."

"Oh, yeah?" The first guy barked. "What's so great about it, hillbilly?"

Komasan narrowed his eyes. "For one, the air is sweet. Not this black muck you folks breathe."

The guys all laughed, but Komasan went on. "And the sky is huge. You can see the stars at night. The people are friendly to everyone. It's a swell place to live . . . especially with a brother like my Komajiro!"

The three guys just laughed.

Something in Komasan snapped. He growled and charged at them, ready to defend his brother, the country life he loved so dearly, and himself.

The guys kept on laughing. But then Komasan tripped and flipped through the air! He hit the first guy in the stomach, knocking him over. Then he bounced onto the second guy's head, pulling off his wig. He landed on the third guy, tearing off his hat.

One by one, Komasan took down the three clubgoers.

"This guy is wack," one guy groaned. The other two just moaned. They staggered to their feet and ran away.

"Brother, you're amazing!" Komajiro said gratefully. "You totally beat those guys! I can't believe you did it!"

Komasan shook his head, dizzy from the fight. "Me neither."

This guy is wack!

"Komasan, you saved me. You're the best brother ever!"

Komajiro put his arm around Komasan, and the two brothers set out into the night.

"Uh . . . you really think so?" Komasan asked.

"I'm so sorry, Komasan. I got it all wrong. I was so dazzled by the big city and all the people that I forgot what's really important," Komajiro said. "I love our home and I love my brother!"

"Komajiro!" Komasan cried.

"I don't need this anymore!" Komajiro said, tossing his phone into the river. "Bye, y'all!"

"Come on, Komasan," he said, hugging his brother tight. "Let's get out of here."

And together, they set off on their next adventure.